I0712764

Juneteenth
This Day Was Made for You and Me

William Teller

Illustrations by Eliza Manzanilla

*"Dedicated to all those who fight for freedom, and wish
to see the world a more just and noble place."*

I remember it clearly, a Monday same as all the rest. Momma and I had awoken in bondage, like the Hebrews of old down in Egyptland.

But just as God delivered them,
He was bringing freedom to us. It
was June 19th, and our
jubilee day had come at last.

It was 1865 and the great big war between North
and South had finally ended in April.
Old President Lincoln was sadly taken from us then
too by an assassin in Ford's Theater. It was one more
loss in a war that had already seen so much tragedy.
But despite all that, things hadn't changed yet for us
down here on Galveston Island.

PEACE AT LAST

Just off the coast of Texas, down the
rail lines from Houston, the island of
Galveston had seen a great naval battle
halfway through the war.
The North had come to set the island
free, but they only held the port for a few
months before it was taken back by the
secesh (a nickname given to those who
had seceded from the Union).

Cannon balls flew into town, hitting the Hendley building.
The damage can still be seen to this day.
The Union flag wouldn't fly over Galveston again until June
1865, two months after the whole war was over.

That June, Major General Gordon Granger sailed into port with 2,000 federal troops. He set up his headquarters at the Osterman Building on The Stand & 22nd street.

The American flag was raised over Galveston Island once more. The waving of those Stars & Stripes had never looked so good.

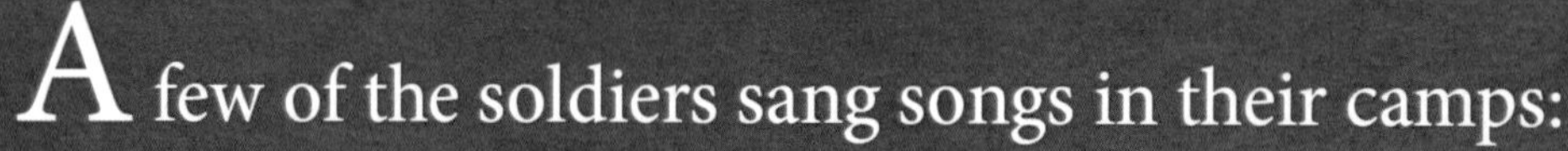

A few of the soldiers sang songs in their camps:

"Hurrah, Hurrah, we bring
the jubilee! Hurrah, Hurrah,
the flag that makes you free!"

"Yes, we'll rally round the flag,
Yes, we'll rally once again!
Shouting the battle cry of Freedom!
And we'll fill our vacant ranks with a
million free men more! Shouting the
battle cry of freedom!"

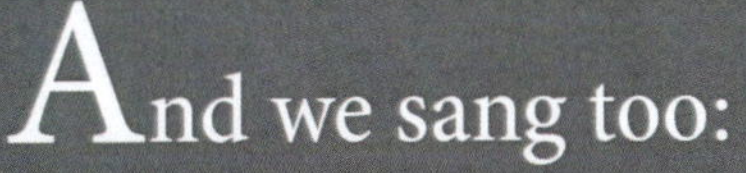

And we sang too:

"I sing because I'm happy, I sing because
I'm free,
For His eye is on the sparrow, and I know
He watches me."

The uncivil war cost the lives of more than six hundred thousand Americans.
The question of slave or free had been going on long before the bloody
battles of Gettysburg, Antietam, and Chickamauga.
And the Union knew why they fought. They knew their cause was one of freedom.

UNKNOWN
U.S.
SOLDIER

UNKNOWN
U.S. SOLDIER

Mamma and me later found out
that there were some in the North
who didn't want to win the war,
but just end it and make peace
with the South.
These northerners were called
Copperheads, but good, old
President Lincoln and General
Sherman knew nothing less than
total victory would set us free and
bring all Americans into the light.

On January 1st, 1863, President Lincoln announced his Emancipation Proclamation, saying that "all persons held as slaves in rebellious states are free." And in January of 1865, the U.S. Congress passed the 13th Amendment, abolishing slavery once and for all in the whole country. But it wouldn't become official law of the land until December of that year.

So, that Monday in June of 1865, when General Granger sent out his Order Number 3 to be posted outside Army H.Q. at the Osterman Building, as well as the U.S. Customs House, and Reedy Chapel, it was made clear: the Union had come to enforce our dearly departed president's proclamation.

In the days of old, every 50th year, God brought His people jubilee.
A year in which debts were forgiven, and slaves were freed.
1865 was our jubilee year. June our jubilee month. The nineteenth our jubilee day.

We'd risen with the sun in bondage, but would welcome the moon delivered. It would take some time for that freedom to fully blossom, but the chains had been loosed, and our march out from Pharaoh's grip had begun.

Celebrations of remembrance began that very next June 19th. We even blended the name together in a *portmanteau*, wherein two words get smooshed together (like *sheep herder*) to become one new word (*shepherd*). From there on out, we called the day Juneteenth. And we've been remembering it ever since.

But this day is more than just for those of us who lived it.
It's a day for all people, everywhere who love freedom and
are committed to fighting the Pharaohs of the world.

As I continue the words of my great, great grandmother, I'm proud to say those celebrations not only haven't stopped, but they've gotten bigger and grander each year. In 1979, Texas lawmaker Al Edwards started a commemorative prayer breakfast and ceremonial reading of General Order Number 3 from the balcony of Ashton Villa, one of the oldest houses in Galveston that dates back before the war.

That next year, thanks to Representative Edwards, Texas made Juneteenth a statewide holiday. And in 2021 it officially became a nationwide holiday for all Americans.

In June of 2020, Edwards' children took over for him, with his son Al Edwards II telling the crowd assembled, "This is not just a Black holiday. It's our day. Juneteenth is everyone's."

So, *what are the colors of Juneteenth?* Red, **White**, and **Blue**. Like the flag designed by the National Juneteenth Celebration Foundation. *Who is Juneteenth for?* For all who want to celebrate freedom, to remember those who fought for it, those who prayed for it, and for all who love and promote freedom today.
Juneteenth is for all of us. It was made for you and me.

9 798988 288831